MW00678575

In the
Shadow of a
Stranger

In the Shadow of a Stranger

by
Judi Wiegman

Beacon Hill Press of Kansas City
Kansas City, Missouri

Copyright 2003
By Beacon Hill Press of Kansas City

Printed in the United States of America

ISBN 083-412-0119

Cover Design: Michael Walsh
Cover Illustration: Dick Wahl
Illustrator: Dick Wahl

Editor: Donna Manning
Assistant Editor: Stephanie Harris

All Scripture quotations are from the *Holy Bible, New International Version®* (NIV®). Copyright © 1973, 1978, 1984 by International Bible Society. Used by permission of Zondervan Publishing House. All rights reserved.

Note: This is a fictional story based on true incidents. It is part of the *Understanding Christian Mission,* Children's Mission Education curriculum. It is designed to correlate with this year's theme, Compassionate Ministries. Lessons focus on how missionaries help people meet their physical, emotional, and spiritual needs.

10   9   8   7   6   5   4   3   2   1

This book is dedicated to Mrs. Priestner and
her sixth grade class at Metroplex Chapel Academy.
They read each chapter, gave me encouragement,
and prayed for me as I wrote this story.

Contents

1

The Adventure Begins

The sound of the jet plane brought me to my feet. "This is the day!" I shouted. I tripped over my shoes and suitcase as I bolted down the hall toward the kitchen. Mom was cooking my favorite breakfast of waffles and sausage.

"Mom! Do you know what day it is?"

"Oh, just another Tuesday." Mom's eyes sparkled as she giggled. "Christian, do you know something I don't know?"

"You're teasing, Mom. Are you ready for our trip to Albania (al-BAY-nee-uh)?"

It had been six years since my adoptive parents brought my sister, Besa (BAY-suh), and me to America from Albania. I am 12 years old now and Besa is 15.

I grabbed mom's spatula from her hand and jumped about the room chanting, "Today we fly to Albania, the country where I was born. Today we . . ."

"What's all the racket about?" Besa interrupted as she and Dad entered the kitchen. "You would think we were going on a trip or something."

Dad grinned as he sat down at the table with his notebook containing all the information about our journey. I plopped down beside him and began to search for the map. I had looked at the map many times. In fact, I had read and studied about Albania. It

is located in Europe on the Balkan (BAWL-kun) Peninsula and lies directly across from Italy on the Adriatic (ay-dree-AT-ik) Sea. It borders Greece on the south and Yugoslavia (yew-goh-SLAH-vee-uh) on the north and east. Albania is just a little larger than the state of Maryland.

I quickly located Europe and placed my finger on Albania. I had traced around the edge of this tiny country many times. This time was different. I realized in less than 48 hours I would be there!

"Mom, tell me again how you and Dad discovered Besa and me and brought us home with you."

"Oh, Christian," Besa retorted, "you've heard that story a hundred times. Mom, please don't tell it now."

"I know you love to hear the story, Christian. But we have several things to do before we leave. I'll tell you the story when we get on the plane. Now eat your breakfast. Waffles will not be on the menu in Albania."

I gobbled down the waffles, stuffed in the sausage, and washed it down with large gulps of cold milk. After breakfast we had family devotions. I could not concentrate on the scriptures Dad read. My mind was elsewhere. "What would it be like to see Albania again? Would I recognize anyone?" I wondered. Sometimes I closed my eyes real tight and thought about Albania, but I couldn't remember very much.

Dad concluded our devotional time with prayer. Mom asked Besa and me to check our bags and help Dad get everything to the car.

As I searched my room to see if there was anything I forgot, I gazed at the mementos on my walls. The ribbons, certificates, photos, and posters represented my life. I was thankful for my friends, my family, and a God who loves me.

"Christian, hurry up," called Mom.

Quickly I double-checked my list and carry-on bag. I saw one more item I wanted to pack. I grabbed a bottle of soap bubbles, slipped it into my backpack, and headed for the car. The adventure was about to begin.

2

A Double-Decker Experience

"Aaaaaah!" I squealed as I caught the first glimpse of our plane sitting on the runway. "Dad, look at that gigantic plane!" Even though we lived near the Dallas-Fort Worth Airport and saw planes fly over our house almost every day, nothing could have prepared me for the incredible sight of this enormous silver jet!

"It's a double-decker!" responded Dad. "We flew in one of these when we brought you here from Albania." Dad looked at Mom and smiled.

"Do you remember, Besa?" I yanked on her arm, but she had a faraway look in her eyes.

"Y-yes," she answered slowly. "I do remember." She glanced at Mom and then added, "I am remembering a lot of things today."

"Me too, Besa." Mom wiped a tear from her eye.

"What's up with you three?" I said impatiently. "Pull yourselves together and let's go. I want to get on that plane."

"Not so fast, young man," Dad chuckled. "We have to check in before we can board the plane."

"Oh, that's right," I said. "Where's my passport?"

I remembered a passport is a legal document that allows a person to travel from one country to another. Airport officials stamp the passport each time it is presented for travel between countries. My parents' passports displayed special stamps from the places they had traveled.

"I have your passport, Son."

Dad handed the passports and tickets to a ticket agent. The man looked directly at me. "So you're going back home?"

"No, sir. We're going back for a visit," I explained.

Dad's voice was strong and firm. "We've turned them into Texans, and we're mighty proud to call them ours."

It seemed to take forever for airport personnel to check our bags and paperwork. Finally we started toward the gate where the huge silver jet waited.

"Christian, look!" Besa exclaimed. "It's Martin, Susan, Tim, and others from our church."

"What a neat surprise," said Mom. "They've come to say good-bye."

While Mom, Dad, and Besa hugged everyone, I talked with my friends. The ladies gave Mom a special journal so she could write about our experiences while in Albania. We joined hands with our friends and prayed together. Then we proceeded to our gate.

❋   ❋   ❋

"Wow!" I exclaimed as we stepped into the plane. My eyes searched every direction.

The flight attendant smiled. "Welcome aboard, young man, young lady. Enjoy your flight today."

"Wow!" It seemed like the only word that would come out of my mouth.

We rounded the corner into the aisle. "Besa, look at all the seats! Come on," I said as I nudged her down the aisle.

"Christian, stop pushing," she said firmly.

Just then, a flight attendant offered to help us find our seats and place our carry-on bags in the compartment above. Besa put all her stuff in the seat next to Mom.

"How can you be so calm at a time like this?" I asked.

"I'm older," teased Besa.

I had never seen the inside of a double-decker plane. It took awhile for everyone to find their seats and get settled. We learned the second level was reserved for business class.

"Besa, Christian, are you listening?" asked Mom. "Fasten your seat belts. We will soon be taking off."

The giant plane gracefully lifted off the runway, and we were airborne. I smashed my face against the window and peered at the figures on the ground. They became harder and harder to distinguish.

"Well, Son, how is everything so far? Are you glad you came along?" Dad teased. I turned and smiled at him. I felt like the luckiest boy on the planet!

Time went by quickly. I was surprised when the "Fasten Seat Belts" sign lit up indicating we were landing in New York. Some passengers had reached their destination and left the plane. Others joined us for our long flight across the Atlantic Ocean.

One of the new passengers was a boy named Mark who was about my age. We quickly became acquainted and made plans to play video games during the long flight ahead of us. Mark had some great games in his carry-on bag that would keep us occupied. With our parents' permission, we made arrangements to sit together.

"Hey, Mark, before we play a game, would you like to hear a story?" I asked.

"What kind of story?" questioned Mark.

"It's a true story about how Besa and I came from Albania to live in America."

"Awesome!" exclaimed Mark. "I sure would."

"Mom tells it best," said Besa. Dad and I looked at Besa, and then we began to laugh.

"Well, I do like to hear the story," admitted Besa.

"OK," agreed Mom. "I did promise."

"Don't leave anything out, Mom. Tell about the rag, the rain, and everything," I said.

"Well, let's see. Where should I begin so Mark will understand? Should I start with the duffel bag?"

3

More than a Mission Trip

"Actually, Mark, my parents brought us home in a duffel bag." I waited for Besa's response. And it was a swift one.

"Christian! You say that every time Mom tells this story. You know better," Besa chided in a sisterly voice.

"Mark, we didn't stick them in a duffel bag. We have all the proper papers to prove they belong to us," Dad replied.

"Let me tell the real story," said Mom. "We were on a mission. A mission in Albania. Our mission was to canvas Shkoder (SHKOH-deŕ), a city in northern Albania."

"That's where I'm from, Mark," I quickly added.

"We planned to share the gospel with every home," continued Mom. "There were 13 of us on the mission team, and we had three weeks to accomplish the mission. We knew God would help us with the plan. But we never dreamed God's plan for us included Christian and Besa. Not in a million years.

"We had been in the city for a few days, had our training sessions, and even learned to say a few words in Albanian—*miremengjes* (meer-uh-MIN-jess) means good morning and *mirupasfshim* (meer-uh-PAHF-shim) means good-bye."

"If you could only say a few words, how did you talk to people?" asked Mark.

"That's a good question, Mark," replied Dad. "We had an interpreter who accompanied us."

"An interpre . . . what?" Mark asked.

Dad chuckled. "An interpreter is someone who speaks more than one language and helps each person understand what the other is saying."

"Oh, I get it," said Mark. "When did you see Christian?"

"Well, one day our team decided to walk through the village and visit some of the shops," said Mom. "A slight mist was falling, and the air was damp, making it quite cool. As we walked along, we heard a whimpering sound. Ahead of us we spotted an old, dirty rag spread out in the middle of the sidewalk. On the rag was a small child in tattered clothes."

"It was Christian," interrupted Besa.

"Yes, it was Christian." Mom had tears in her eyes. "My heart hurt when I first saw him. He looked so cold and lonely. I could not understand why he was just lying there."

"As people walked by, they dropped coins on the rag," explained Dad. "Two people from our group placed some fruit beside him."

"Besa, where were you?" asked Mark.

"I was watching from behind a tree," answered Besa.

"Yes, the most unusual thing happened," Mom continued. "A girl in ragged clothes suddenly darted across the street, grabbed the coins and fruit, and disappeared again behind a tree."

"I was watching him carefully so nothing would happen to him," explained Besa. "Then I saw you, Mom. You began to cry as you looked at him."

"I could not believe my eyes!" Mom said. "Lydia, our interpreter, told us Besa and Christian were street children. She said they had to beg and steal to get food! I slowly knelt beside Christian. Besa crept from behind the tree and watched me."

"I-I had never seen anyone so kind before," remarked Besa. "When I saw her kneel beside Christian, I felt warm inside. She reached out her hand to me and I touched it. I wondered why I wasn't afraid. She smiled at me and said, *'miremengjes.'* I was so surprised."

Mom hugged Besa. "I felt something wonderful was about to happen. I couldn't erase that scene from my mind. We were concerned about Christian and Besa's welfare—whether they were warm enough and had enough food. We prayed and asked God how we could help them.

"During breakfast the next morning, we told the missionary about Christian and Besa. We asked if the government allowed street children to be taken out of Albania."

"Since Communists no longer rule, some people have been given permission to take children to live in other countries," explained the missionary. "I will contact someone to find out what's involved."

"We were content with that answer," said Mom. "We left the apartment, joined our team, and continued visiting the homes of people in the city."

❊　❊　❊

"The missionary informed us the next day that Besa and Christian were indeed street children. But unlike some street children," said Mom, "they lived with their mother's relative in a crowded little house on the edge of town. She had three children of her own and took care of two other street children. The children helped by begging for food and money, which is common in Albania."

"Oh, Christian, that must have been tough," said Mark.

"It was!" I exclaimed. "But the story isn't over."

"The good part is yet to come," added Besa.

"Yes," agreed Dad. "That afternoon our missionary friend took us to the house where Besa and Christian lived and introduced us to their relative. We began to visit Besa and Christian every day."

"I looked forward to your visits," said Besa. "I loved the kind look in your eyes."

"Because of the relative's situation, she agreed to let us take Besa and Christian to America. She felt they would have a better life," Mom said.

"When I found out we were going to America with you," Besa said, "I was very excited. I didn't like the way we had to live."

As Mom continued the story about the stacks of paperwork they filled out and filed for our release, I drifted to sleep.

4

Sightseeing

The wheels touched down on the runway, and the plane taxied toward the gate.

"Are we here already?" I rubbed my eyes and tried to focus.

"We're in Amsterdam (AM-ster-dam), a beautiful, old city in the Netherlands," Dad said as he ruffled my hair. "Say good-bye to Mark. We have to collect our suitcases and go through Customs. Then we can go sightseeing."

We rode the train downtown and spent the day visiting old churches and other buildings. We took a boat ride through town to see shops that are built right on a canal. Mom and Besa loved it! I must admit, it was neat.

"Dad, why are there so many bikes in this city?" I asked.

"Many people ride bikes to work," he replied. "Many others walk. You notice there aren't many cars here. The streets in these old cities are too narrow for cars."

The next morning we boarded another plane. Before we knew it, we were in Athens, Greece.

As we stepped out of the plane, Besa gave a huge sigh. "We are almost home."

Dad smiled. "That's right. Tomorrow we'll be there."

"That's tomorrow. What about today?" I wondered.

Just then Dad said, "Christian, as soon as we get

settled in the hotel, let's go to the arcade I told you about. You and I can play games and the girls can shop."

"Great idea, Dad!"

We crowded into a taxi and headed for the hotel. What a ride! Dad pointed at the speedometer. We were riding in an old Mercedes, but we were cruisin'! The driver wove in and out of traffic at 60 miles an hour! No one said a word. We just hung on.

"Well," Mom began as the driver left, "can you believe that ride? Did you see how fast we were going? Why didn't you say something?" She looked at Dad and waited for a response.

"Cool!" I exclaimed.

"Most fun we've had so far, right, Son?" Dad replied with a twinkle in his eye.

As we entered the hotel, Dad exclaimed, "Oh no! I left the camera bag in the cab!"

"Are you sure?" Mom questioned. "You know we hid some of our money in there. We'll never see that bag again."

"You're probably right," agreed Dad. "But, let's stop over here and pray."

We joined hands and Dad prayed.

"Is this yours?" someone called. We looked up to see the cab driver holding our camera bag. He reached out and shook Dad's hand. Dad smiled as he handed the man a reward for his honesty. As quickly as he came, the driver left.

We headed to our room. Once inside, we thanked God for our safe trip and the honest cab driver. Then we were off to the arcade.

Dad and I played games for what seemed like hours while the girls went shopping. When they returned, they announced they were hungry.

"Can you find that restaurant?" Mom inquired. "You know, the one that serves pork chops and french fries with that special sauce."

"I've already asked the hotel clerk." Dad grinned. "However, it means another cab ride. Are you two up for it?" he teased.

"Well," said Mom, nodding at Besa. "I guess we can handle it. I really would like those pork chops."

"Then it's settled," said Dad.

We ate in the same restaurant where Mom and Dad had eaten six years ago. The only thing on their menu was pork chops and french fries, and they were good! I gobbled down more than my share of the fries served with white sauce—not ketchup.

Back at the hotel I quickly prepared for bed. Tomorrow was the BIG day. We would leave Greece and head north to Albania, at last!

5

An Unscheduled Stop

"That man keeps staring at me," I whispered to Besa on the plane.

"Shhh," she replied. "I know. He's been staring at me too. Don't look at him."

"He looks like us. Do you think he's Albanian?" I questioned.

Besa grabbed my arm. "Be quiet. Don't draw attention to yourself."

"Hey, what are you mumbling about?" Dad inquired. But he didn't wait for our answer. "That's strange, I think we're landing. We weren't scheduled to stop anyplace else. What's going on?"

"Look," Mom said as she pointed out the window. "The name on that building says Thessalonica (THEH-suh-lah-nie-kuh)."

Just then we heard a voice on the speaker. "Ladies and gentlemen, we have landed in Thessalonica. Please enter the terminal and be prepared to show your passports."

"What's wrong?" I asked.

"They've found out about us," teased Besa.

"That's not funny," I replied.

"It's OK," Dad reassured us. "You'll be just fine. We'll all be just fine."

The officials checked and stamped all passports as we entered the terminal. No one said much and no questions were asked.

"Look," Besa whispered, "they're taking that man into another room."

"What man?" I questioned.

"You know, the one who was staring at us," she replied.

Through the glass, I could see the man sitting at a table.

"What are you whispering about?" This time Dad waited for our answer.

But we both just stared at him and shook our heads. Then Besa slowly began to explain. "Well, do you see that man in there? Well, he kept watching us on the plane. Now they're asking him questions."

"Don't worry," Dad tried to comfort us. "I have no idea what's happening. But everything will be all right."

Suddenly an officer emerged from the room. "You may return to the plane," he said.

As the plane lifted off the ground, I looked around at each passenger. "I don't see that man," I whispered to Besa.

"He's not on the plane," she whispered back to me.

"Are you sure?" I scanned the plane again, then turned to Dad. "I don't see the stranger."

"I know, Son," he responded. "I know. They detained the man at the terminal. I knew you would soon realize that."

"Do you realize where we've been?" Mom asked, and then proceeded to tell us. "We stopped in Thessalonica!"

"What about it, Mom?" I asked.

"Well, it's thrilling!" exclaimed Mom. "We've been in the city where Paul traveled as a missionary. On his second missionary journey, Paul founded the first church in Thessalonica, the capital of Macedonia. When he was forced to leave, he sent Timothy to check on the church he had started. From Corinth he wrote the First Book of Thessalonians to encourage young Christians. Many scholars think it was written about 20 years after Jesus ascended into heaven."

"Your mom is right." Dad continued, "Just think, we made an unscheduled stop in a very important city. It is one of the oldest, continuously settled communities in the world."

"This was all very interesting," I thought. But it didn't make me forget about the stranger. I shivered as I thought about his watching us. Dad said not to worry. After all, the man was in Thessalonica now, and that was the end of it.

6

Our Journey to Shkoder

"All right!" I exclaimed as we landed in Tirana (ti-RAH-nuh). "We're here!" I shouted, in case someone had not noticed. I pressed my face against the window to take in every detail.

Dad caught a glimpse of Ginny and the other missionaries waving. They waited patiently while we were cleared through Customs. Then we collected our bags and headed out the door. Several children with outstretched, dirty hands crowded around us.

"That's what we used to do," Besa cried. "I remember. It makes me sad to see them."

Mom put her arm around Besa. "I understand."

"You will probably remember other things about your life here," said Dad. "Just remember this, you are part of our family, and we will take you home with us. I promise."

Those words from Dad made us feel better. Although I was excited, I was a little uneasy. Everything seemed so strange, yet so familiar. I was relieved when we were safely in Ginny's car.

The journey north to Shkoder was long. While my parents talked with their friends, Besa and I gazed out the windows and took in every sight along the way.

Suddenly, Besa shook my arm. "Look, Christian," she squealed. "A cart full of leeks!"

On the narrow winding road in front of us was a horse-drawn cart. In the back was a pile of long white vegetables with green leaves.

"Leeks?" I questioned. "What are they?" As Ginny swerved to pass the cart, Besa rolled down my window. A strong smell reached my nose, and I yelled, "Onions! They smell like onions!"

Everyone in the car had a good laugh. I plugged my nose and laughed too.

"Good one, Besa," Dad said, as he gave Besa a high five.

"Yessss!" exclaimed Besa. "They taste like onions, but are still very different. They are especially good with rice."

"I'm not eating them," I declared. "They smell terrible!"

"Well," Dad chuckled, "I'm sure the smell of the horse-drawn cart didn't help. You might change your mind if you tasted them."

As our car approached the top of a hill, Ginny slowed down and stopped. "This is a good place to get out and stretch for a moment," she said. "You can see Shkoder in the valley below us."

I leaped from the car and strained my eyes to look at Shkoder in the distance. It was beautiful!

"Christian, see the mountains over there beyond the city?" asked Dad. "That is the border of Yugoslavia."

"For real?" I asked.

"Yes," Dad replied. "Let me give you a little history about this area. The Book of Acts tells about Paul's vision. He saw a man begging him to come to Macedonia and help the people (Acts 16:9). At that time, all of this area was known as Macedonia. But, Paul did not enter this land that is now Albania. That's why your mother and I felt so privileged to come here with our mission team. We were continuing the journey Paul started."

"Yes," Ginny added, "the Church of the Nazarene organized its work here in 1991, just before your parents came. Now we have a well-established church."

"Well, enough history. We must continue our journey," Mom said. "I am more excited than ever to get there."

We piled back in the car. I leaned my head against the window and tried to imagine what my life would have been like if the Church of the Nazarene had not come to my country. I was glad to have a new life in Christ!

Suddenly we stopped in front of the apartment building where we would be staying. "A *pallati* (pah-LAH-tee)!" my sister squealed. *Pallati* was a name given to apartment buildings by the Communists. Translated, it means palace! It was their way of making the people think they lived in luxury even though they did not.

"It's pink!" I exclaimed.

"Yes," Mom laughed. "They have three colors of paint in Albania. Pink, turquoise, and orange. It looks like THAT hasn't changed."

"And," Dad added, "they sometimes use all three in one room. You'll see."

Luckily, we were on the second floor. Each apartment building is five stories high. But they have NO elevators, just stairways.

We got everything settled in the small, crowded apartment we would call home for the next two weeks. I decided to go outside and look around. In my pocket, I carefully placed the last item I had packed. I was ready to go.

7

Bubbles and Giggles

The boy slowly approached from the other side of the courtyard-like area. As he walked, he kicked at the dirt and chunks of metal and broken glass left there by wars fought years ago.

"*Miredita, si jeni?* (How are you?)" I called. I stood up from the large rock where I sat next to our apartment. Then I carefully reached in my pocket to retrieve my treasure.

The boy replied, "*Jam mire.* (I am fine.) *Si e ke emrin?* (What is your name?)" he continued.

"Christian," I replied as I removed the lid from my treasure. I dipped my bubble stick into the solution and began blowing large, beautiful bubbles.

The boy began chasing the bubbles and trying to catch them. Soon there was a crowd of children giggling and chasing bubbles. It worked!

Mom had told me she used bubbles to communicate with the children when she couldn't speak their language. She said it always drew a crowd.

All of a sudden, I saw an older girl walking toward me with a puzzled look.

"I've seen bubbles like these before," she said in English. "Do I know you?"

"How would you know me?" I asked.

"My name is Lydia. Years ago a lady came from America. She had bubbles. I was her interpreter. Is the lady here? Are you Christian? Is Besa here?" she asked.

"Yes, yes to all your questions. Come on!" I called. "I'll take you to them."

"Mom, Dad, Besa!" I yelled. "Look who I found! She saw me blowing bubbles, and she remembered you, Mom!"

"Lydia!" Mom exclaimed. Everyone hugged and cried and laughed.

Suddenly Mom turned and stared at me. "What bubbles? You brought bubbles?" she asked.

"Yup," I responded. "And it worked just like you said. I started blowing bubbles, and all the kids came. Then I saw Lydia."

"Well, aren't you the clever one." Dad gave me a high five. "Good work, Son. Good work."

Lydia shared how her family had become Christians with the help of our missionaries in Albania. My parents had many questions. Finally, Besa and Lydia disappeared into the other room. I decided to continue my adventure outside. Did I say adventure? Little did I know what waited for me this time.

8

Strange Sightings

"Besa!" I yelled, "I-I saw him!"

"Who, Christian, who are you talking about?" she quizzed.

"You know. The man on the plane. The one who kept staring at us. The one we left behind. *The stranger!*"

Besa quickly told Lydia about the man. The three of us nearly tripped each other as we raced downstairs and out of the apartment. But no one was there.

"Maybe it just looked like him," Besa said.

"Nope! I saw him!" I exclaimed.

Besa and Lydia just looked at each other, shrugged, and went back into the apartment. I followed them, insisting that I really had seen the stranger. They disappeared through the door, giggling.

"What's up, Son?" Dad inquired.

"Nothing," I replied. I was embarrassed to tell him. What if I was wrong?

"Well, I have exciting news about tomorrow," said Dad. "We are going to visit the old castle—the one situated on that high rock formation, just outside the city."

"Oh, wow!" I immediately thought of knights and prancing horses. I quickly forgot about the stranger.

The next morning we were up with the sun and on a bus headed for the edge of town. Once we ar-

rived, we started the long trek up the winding dirt road to the old castle.

The ancient castle had been built during medieval times, an 800-year period of history extending from the 7th to the 15th century A.D. (anno Domini, which means after Christ.)

When Dad gave Besa and me permission to explore, we didn't need to be told twice.

"Hey, Besa, check it out!" I shouted as we descended the dark stairs. "Look! A real dungeon with bars and everything!"

"This is way cool," Besa replied. "Let's take pictures of each other. Our friends will never believe this!" I put on my most distressed look, and Besa laughed as she snapped picture after picture of me.

We could only imagine all the events that took place in this ancient castle. We climbed the narrow winding stairs leading almost straight up in the round turret. From the top of the tower we could see the entire city spread out below us. This fortress was built in a perfect location. The enemy who might have tried to storm this castle would have been seen.

For a while I pretended to be a knight. An old piece of wood made a worthy sword. I chopped at the air to protect "our" castle from bad guys. Two words from my sister's mouth stopped my quest.

The stranger! Besa shouted as she pointed her finger toward a small courtyard below us.

I ran to her side just in time to see the mysterious stranger looking in our direction. We slumped behind the short brick wall and froze. "Did he hear me?" Besa stared at me. "He looked this way."

"I told you I saw him yesterday. Now do you believe me? I don't know if he saw us. I wonder who he is?"

Slowly we poked our heads up and peered over the brick wall. It was him all right. He was with several other people. They were all crowded around him looking at something in his hand.

"What are they doing, Besa?"

"Come on," Besa whispered. "Let's get out of here. It's almost time to meet Mom and Dad in the outer court." We scrambled down the stairs and in the opposite direction of the stranger. We were out of breath when we rounded the corner and relieved to see our parents there to meet us.

"You look like you saw a ghost," Dad laughed and gave us both a hug as we tried to catch our breath.

"Yes, uh, Dad," I stammered, "we just saw the mysterious stranger. You know, the man who got off the plane in Thessalonica and didn't get back on."

"Yeah," Besa added. "And Christian saw him yesterday too."

"Is that so?" Dad questioned. "Well, maybe he lives here or has business here. Don't worry about him. Stay close to me, and point him out if you see him again. Now it's time to take the bus back to the city. Did you have fun?"

"Oh yeah, Dad, it was a blast!" I gave the thumbs up sign.

"We have pictures to prove it," added Besa.

"Christian, I'll race you to the bottom of the hill," invited Dad.

"Besa, you stay close to Mom. We'll meet you at the bus. Come on, Christian. Ready, set, go!"

We were panting when we reached the bottom of the hill. We climbed on the bus and flopped into our seats. This was enough excitement for one day. I was glad to be going back to our apartment. When everyone was seated, the bus began to jerk away from the curb.

"Look, Dad, look!" Besa squealed. Dad looked up just in time to catch a glimpse of the stranger coming down the trail toward the bus stop.

"Did you see him? Did you?" I questioned.

"Yes, I saw him," Dad replied. "We can't do anything about it now. Besides, we have no reason to question the man. He hasn't done anything."

"I know." I slumped in my seat. "At least you saw him. We all saw him."

9

A Wrong Turn

The next morning something strange and wonderful happened. I woke to a smell that seemed new, yet familiar; it was the smell of fresh bread baking. I took a deep breath. Suddenly, I knew! I remembered a day when someone brought freshly baked bread to my relative's house. I'll never forget the smell of that bread!

Leaping from my bed, I darted into the living room. "Mom, I remember the fresh bread!"

"Christian, that's a wonderful memory," she said as she put her arm around me. Then Dad and Besa joined us.

"Dad, may I go get some fresh baked bread?" I waited for his answer.

"Yes. You may go. The bakery is two blocks down the street and around the corner," Dad explained.

Dad put the *lek* [LEK] (Albanian money) in my hand and sent me out the door. As I trudged along, I felt a sense of pride. Someone had done this for me. Now, I wanted to do the same for my family.

The morning was quiet. Too quiet. Something was missing.

"That's it," I said to myself. "No birds. Mom was right." She told me that was one of the first things she noticed in Albania. Someone explained that birds only live in the mountains. That did not matter to me because I had a mission to accomplish today.

After I bought the bread, I started walking toward

the apartment. Suddenly the street looked different to me. Did I make a wrong turn? Where was I? I turned around and headed back the way I came, deciding to follow my nose to the bakery.

As I rounded the corner, I ran into a man coming out of the bakery. I landed on the ground with the bread in my lap. "Sorry, Sir." I apologized as I tried to get up. "Oh no! You. I mean, oh no!" I was staring straight at the mysterious stranger!

"Hey, young fella," he began. "Are you OK? Say, do I know you?"

"Me?" I questioned. "I-I, we, er. I don't think so." The man chuckled at my response.

"I-I gotta go," I stammered.

"Dad! Dad!" I shouted. In the distance I could see Dad coming down the sidewalk with a worried look on his face.

"Christian, you took too long. I came out to look for you," he said as he glanced at the stranger.

"I made a wrong turn. I'm OK. But I'm glad to see you." I glanced in the direction of the man.

Dad reached toward the stranger to shake hands. "I'm Rev. Thompson, sir," he began. "Do I know you?"

"Hello," the stranger responded. "My name is Anton Duka. I'm pleased to meet you. You also look familiar to me in some way. Have we met before?"

"Well," a smile spread across Dad's face, "I think we have met. Let's sit down on this bench. I think I finally have this mystery figured out. This is my son, Christian." I listened carefully as Dad revealed the identity of the mysterious stranger.

"Six years ago my wife and I came here on a mission trip. We met a young man named Anton. He was a street boy who also cared for his four-year-old nephew. Could that have been you?"

Tears welled up in the man's eyes. "That was me all right!"

"Wow! I can't believe this!" I exclaimed.

"We are staying near here. Do you have time to come with us to the apartment?" asked Dad. "We have some catching up to do."

"Yes. That would be good," Anton agreed. "Let's go."

I could hardly wait until we reached the apartment. What would Besa say?

I burst into the apartment with the whole story. "Mom, Besa, I got lost and went back and bumped into the stranger and Dad came and . . ."

"Slow down," Dad chuckled. "Sarah, Besa, do we have a surprise for you!"

10

The Truth Revealed

"Sarah," Dad looked at Mom. "This is Anton. Do you remember?"

"Anton?" Mom moved closer to the man we had called the stranger. "Anton!" Mom exclaimed.

"Anton?" Besa was trying to remember too. "Anton and Edon?"

"Yes, yes! You remember me. While we were street kids, I took care of Edon just like you cared for Christian. When your parents came to Albania, we followed them around. They gave us food and clothes. They showed great compassion to the street kids."

"Hey," I interrupted. "Wait a minute. What about Thessalonica? We saw you on the plane. You kept staring at us. You didn't get back on the plane. What happened?"

"Christian!" Besa chided. "Don't be rude."

Anton chuckled. "That's all right, Christian. I was staring. I thought I knew you, but I couldn't remember where I'd seen you. And about Thessalonica. I was returning from a business trip, and some of my papers were questioned. The officials detained me until they could check them out. It happens quite often here."

"You sure had these two interested," laughed Dad. "In fact, they became more interested each time they saw you. When they spotted you at the castle yesterday, they were quite sure you were following them."

By now, we were all laughing, and I was very embarrassed.

"I was at the castle yesterday, but I wasn't spying
on you. I shared the gospel with a few people and
prayed with them," Anton explained.

"Anton, do you remember the shoes?" Mom
asked.

"I sure do. Christian, your mom and the others on
the mission team were concerned about us because we
were barefoot. I guess they didn't notice most Albanian
children were barefoot! Anyway, they bought us tennis
shoes. The next day we had huge blisters on both
heels. Your mom cleaned our feet and put medicine
and Band-Aids on them. It was quite an experience."

"And remember the clothes?" Dad asked. "The
teenagers bought new clothes for you, but you wouldn't
wear them."

"That's right," Anton said. "If we wore new
clothes, no one would give us the money we begged
for on the street."

"What happened to Edon? Where is he now?"
Mom asked.

"Edon was adopted by a family from Greece,"
Anton answered. "I was too old for adoption, but I was
happy for Edon. I see him when I go to Greece on
business.

"I often think about the group from America and
will never forget your compassion. One of the teenagers on your team led me to accept Christ as my
personal Savior. You left me with hope for the future.
When Edon was adopted, I began to search for a way
to share what was in my heart. I met with some other
people from the Church of the Nazarene in Tirana."

"Wow! So you're a Christian instead of a spy," I
interrupted.

"Christian!" Besa gave me an annoyed look.

"Yes, Christian," Anton chuckled. "Right now I'm in Shkoder to establish a compassionate ministries center like the one in Tirana."

"That is incredible," Mom replied. "We volunteer at a compassionate ministries center at home. Besa and Christian help too."

Anton stayed with us all morning, and we shared many memories.

11

Discoveries

"Oh, can we, Dad? Will you let me come?" I pleaded. Anton had invited Dad and me to take a walk around town and look for a suitable building for the compassionate ministries center.

"I would be glad to help you find a building," Dad replied. "Christian, you're welcome to come."

As we walked along the sidewalk, Dad pointed out the shop where he had bought Mom a quilt six years earlier. He showed us the orphanage where the teams met in the afternoon. But he stopped right in front of a small coffee shop.

"I remember this place," he began. "The store-keeper let us meet here in the mornings to plan our day. He would play our Christian tapes. Sometimes we could hear the music playing even when we weren't in the shop."

"I remember," Anton said. "He even played the tapes after your team was gone. I would come and sit outside the shop and listen. I missed you very much. Oh, look!" Anton pointed across the street at an empty building with a "For Lease" sign hanging on the door. We hurried across the street for a closer look.

"I remember this place too," Dad said. "One morning while we were in the coffee shop, we saw three young people standing here in front of this building."

"I remember too," Anton said. "They were holding hands and praying."

"That's right, Anton," Dad continued. "They were visiting from Canada. They told us how God had led them to Albania to pray throughout the city of Shkoder. They chose this building as a prayer site because it had once been the home of a former Communist officer."

"That's scary," I said.

"There's nothing to be scared about now, Christian," Anton replied. "Communism is gone from Albania, and new things are happening. This might be the perfect building."

The storekeeper from across the street joined us on the sidewalk. He began speaking to Anton in Albanian.

Anton explained that the storekeeper owned the building and was willing to rent it to him. The storekeeper opened the door and allowed us to go in. After we looked around, he invited us across the street to his coffee shop. We sat around a small table while Dad and Anton discussed the storekeeper's offer. Anton interpreted for Dad, and once or twice he let me help. It was fun to use my Albanian in Albania. Anton made me feel quite grown-up and important.

The men finished their business and shook hands. We headed for the apartment. On the way we found an ice-cream vendor, not a common sight in Albania. We stopped to enjoy a special treat.

"Dad, we should bring Mom and Besa here for ice cream."

"Great idea!" agreed Dad.

I raced up the stairs to the apartment anxious to tell Mom and Besa about our afternoon. "You wouldn't believe all the places we went," I said as I tried to catch my breath. "I saw the coffee shop, the quilt shop, the orphanage, and an old Communist building.

Anton might rent it. Oh, yes, and we stopped for ice cream!"

"Whoa! Slow down," Mom instructed. "I guess you had a good time." She glanced at Dad and Anton. "Find anything?"

They shook their heads, and we burst out laughing. Dad's head was going up and down, and Anton's head was going from left to right. You see, in Albania 'yes' is expressed by shaking your head left to right and 'no' by bobbing up and down. They were both right! But they looked silly.

Anton explained, "We found a building, and I think it is suitable for what we need. I will take my report back to Tirana, and we will see what the missionaries say."

"Good," Mom replied. "We were praying for you. We will continue to ask God to help you with this project."

Anton stood to leave. "I must be going. Thank you for this time together." As he moved toward the door, Besa and I moved with him. There was something so special about seeing him.

Besa spoke first. "Are you leaving soon? For Tirana, I mean?" She glanced toward Mom as she waited for Anton to answer.

"I am scheduled to be back in Tirana on Thursday, but I will be here tomorrow."

"Do you have plans tomorrow?" Dad questioned.

We looked at Mom. "I think they want to know if you can spend the day with us."

Anton chuckled, "I don't have plans. I would love to spend the day with you. Do you have a plan?"

"Yes, yes!" Besa said enthusiastically. "We are going to visit the spot where Mom and Dad first saw us on the street, and then we are going to the mountains for a picnic, and then . . ."

Dad laughed. "I think he gets the picture. Anton, if that sounds good to you, a family outing I mean, meet us here in the morning at eight o'clock. We have borrowed a car so we can go to the mountains."

Anton shook Dad's hand up and down and thanked him over and over. I glanced at Besa. I was pleased she came up with the idea for tomorrow, and her smile told me she was too.

12

A Day with Anton

All night long I kept waking up. Was it morning yet? Finally, six o'clock came! I jumped out of bed and got ready for the day. I heard Mom rattling dishes in the kitchen and hurried to see if she was ready to go.

"*Miremengjes,*" she said with a smile.

"*Miremengjes,*" I replied. "I love to hear you greet me in Albanian. Especially in Albania!"

"You must be as excited as your sister. She is already out on the steps waiting for Anton."

I hurried to join Besa on the porch. "Besa, I thought morning would never come."

"You got that right," she said. "I had a difficult time getting to sleep. It was like the night we left Texas." Besa paused. "Can you believe all that has happened?"

"I can't wait to tell my friends about our trip!" I said excitedly.

"No problem!" She joked. "You'll tell them everything at once."

We were scuffling with each other when we heard Anton. "*Miremengjes,*" he called, as he joined us on the steps.

Besa glanced at her watch. "Glad to see you are early. Maybe our parents will hurry now that you're here." We headed for the door.

"Shhh," I told the others as we noisily entered the apartment. "They're praying."

We stopped in our tracks and waited quietly as Dad finished his prayer for a good day and our safe travel. We all chimed in with a loud "Amen."

"Now can we go?" I prodded.

"Well, I have everything ready for the day," answered Mom.

"OK. Let's go." Dad declared the day's activities officially started.

I was the first one out the door. After we loaded the car, Dad began to drive down one street after another. "Stop!" Besa shouted. "This is the street!"

"You're right, Besa. This is the street," agreed Dad.

We got out of the car and followed Besa. She stopped in front of an old, metal door. She began to cry.

"This is the spot," she said through her tears. "This is where you found us."

"It hasn't changed," Mom commented. "The door is still Albanian pink!" This turned Besa's tears to laughter.

"Let's pray right here," suggested Anton. We reached for each other's hands, formed a tight circle, and bowed our heads. Anton's prayer was perfect. He prayed in Albanian and in English. As Anton said "Amen," we looked up to discover we had attracted a crowd. Several storekeepers had come out of their shops, and other people had stopped nearby.

Anton did not waste any time gathering the people together. He told them who we were and what we were doing there.

"Give him a crowd, and he becomes a preacher!" Dad grinned. "I believe God is going to use Anton in this town."

People began to ask questions. I wondered if any of the storekeepers had been here six years ago. I wondered if they remembered us. Anton passed out a pamphlet about the church and promised to return.

As we got back in the car, Dad thanked God for an opportunity to share His love.

"I know it was God's plan for me to be in Shkoder the very same week you planned to be here," said Anton. "The people were amazed to hear the story of Besa and Christian and actually see them! This will have an impact on our work here."

"Dad," Besa said, "before we leave, would you take some pictures of us on this spot?"

"I would love to take more pictures to add to our family album. Come on, everybody out of the car! Let's do it!"

We took pictures in every combination possible! We even got a storekeeper to take one of all of us. Finally, we got back in the car and headed for the mountains.

Funny, I can't remember the trip up the mountain. I remember resting my head on Anton's shoulder. The next thing I heard was Besa giggling as she shook me awake. "Hey, Sleepyhead," she teased. "We are here! Time to wake up!"

"Huh? I must have dozed off," I explained. Everyone laughed, and Anton teased me until Mom came to the rescue.

"Hope you're all hungry," Mom said. "This is a beautiful spot for a picnic. Listen, everyone."

We stayed very quiet for a moment. "Birds! Listen to the birds!" exclaimed Dad.

"Anton, our mom loves to hear the birds," Besa said. "She is probably the only visitor to Albania who noticed there aren't any in the city! Someone told her she'd have to go to the mountains to hear them."

"And now I have! Thanks," said Mom.

After we ate, we spent time finding trails and exploring the mountain area. All too soon Dad said it was time to begin our journey back to Shkoder.

13

Saying Good-bye

"Good-bye, Anton." We watched Anton disappear down the sidewalk. We were sad to see him leave, but we knew we'd see him one more time in Tirana.

"God is so good." Dad almost sang the words. "I think God led us here to meet Anton. Christian, it was no accident when you bumped into him by the bakery. He needed to locate a building and return to Tirana as soon as possible. God allowed us to be part of this exciting adventure."

During the next few days we visited places around town that Mom and Dad wanted us to see before leaving. We saw a cemetery where the crosses had been knocked off the graves by the Communist soldiers and wired back after Communism was gone. We saw a dome-shaped cement bunker built to house a soldier and his gun during World War II. We visited an orphanage and were reminded that many children still need homes.

All too soon we were on the plane headed back to Texas. I pressed my face against the glass to get one last glimpse of my homeland. "Would I ever return?" I wondered. Deep in my heart, I felt I would. Perhaps one day I would return to work in the compassionate ministries center with Anton.

Right now I was content, very content. I whispered a prayer thanking God for my friends, family, and home. I could hardly wait to see my friends at home. I had so many neat experiences to share with them.

As I reflected on our trip, I could hear Mom and Dad talking in the seat behind us.

"Anton asked if we had plans to return to Albania," Dad said.

"What did you tell him?" asked Mom.

"I told him I would be in contact with him through Compassionate Ministries. And if there was an opportunity, we would come back to lend a hand."

Besa and I gave each other a "high five." We would pray for that opportunity! In the meantime, we knew God wanted us to show compassion to others, just as others had shown compassion to us.